This book belongs to

_____

_____

Look out for other Piccolo and Annabelle books:

A Disastrous Party
The Stinky Cheese Gypsies

Piccolo and Annabelle

VOLUME ONE

A VERY MESSY

INSPECTION

WRITTEN AND ILLUSTRATED BY

STEPHEN AXELSEN

OXFORD
UNIVERSITY PRESS

OXFORD
UNIVERSITY PRESS

Great Clarendon Street, Oxford OX2 6DP

Oxford University Press is a department of the University of Oxford.
It furthers the University's objective of excellence in research, scholarship,
and education by publishing worldwide in

Oxford   New York

Auckland   Cape Town   Dar es Salaam   Hong Kong   Karachi
Kuala Lumpur   Madrid   Melbourne   Mexico City   Nairobi
New Delhi   Shanghai   Taipei   Toronto

With offices in

Argentina   Austria   Brazil   Chile   Czech Republic   France   Greece
Guatemala   Hungary   Italy   Japan   Poland   Portugal   Singapore
South Korea   Switzerland   Thailand   Turkey   Ukraine   Vietnam

Oxford is a registered trade mark of Oxford University Press
in the UK and in certain other countries

First published in 2004 by Random House Australia Pty Ltd, Sydney, Australia.
This edition published by arrangement with Random House Australia

First published in the UK in 2006

British Library Cataloguing in Publication Data

Data available

ISBN-13: 978-0-19-272609-4
ISBN-10: 0-19-272609-9

1 3 5 7 9 10 8 6 4 2

Printed and bound by Mackays of Chatham plc, Chatham, Kent

For Jennifer, my singing, chainsawing seraph.

CONTENTS

'Holywell', No. 9 Pleasant Crescent

CHAPTER ONE
On a Grey Afternoon

Piccolo Grande, a boy aged nine, lived alone in a fine old house at the end of a long gravel driveway. He carefully tended the gardens there and his special fish pond. He washed his dishes, brushed and flossed his teeth, and did his homework on time and sometimes early. In the morning he quietly got himself off to school and came home again in the afternoon.

Now, you may be thinking, What a dull, boring and lonely life! But Piccolo, being a thoughtful and well-organized sort of boy, did not mind too much. Although sometimes he was a little lonely and sad.

He became sad when he thought about his dear missing parents. It was now eighteen months since they had disappeared. Their yacht, the *Leaping Susan*, had sailed into a thick, mysterious mist somewhere in the tropics. They had not been heard of again. Most people thought that they had perished. Piccolo did not. Day by day he lived carefully in his fine house and waited for them to come home. He knew they would. He was sure of it, as sure as the sun rose and set again. Often he would sit with his toes in the perch pond, his most special place, staring at the passing clouds. He could see his parents, Peter and Marjorie Grande, living happily enough on a deserted island, but missing their boy terribly.

One grey Saturday afternoon Piccolo was upstairs thoughtfully sorting old postage stamps into tidy piles. He had weeded the long gravel driveway and finished ironing his handkerchiefs in the morning, and this was his time to relax. As he tidied a pile of rare Lithuanian stamps, an unusual sound passed through the curtains. *Ffffwwwunnngh,* it went, *fffwwwunnngh*; a sort of grunting flapping sound which seemed to be getting closer. As Piccolo watched, a round pink object bobbed into view. He left Lithuania to stand at the window. The thing seemed to be flying with a great effort, just clearing the tree-tops. Piccolo's eyes widened as it came closer. It was a person, furiously beating small feathered wings and carrying two bulky floral bags.

No, I'm not seeing this, thought Piccolo. There was a crunching thud of breaking branches and the sound of falling fruit as the thing flew directly into a pear tree.

No, that didn't happen, Piccolo decided. I must have had too much sun, weeding the drive. That's it. Sunstroke.

He sat back down to his tidy piles—Romania,

An unusual sound passed through the curtains.

Bulgaria, how did this Russian one get into Latvia? . . . until the doorbell rang.

'No, that's not the doorbell.'

But it was, and after a full two minutes of ringing and a high voice calling 'Yoo-hoo!' Piccolo left his desk and walked slowly downstairs. Warily he opened the front door.

'HELLO, PICCOLO!' yelled a breathless little lady. 'Did you get my letter?!' A red round face grinned at him.

Pear twigs were poking out of her wild red hair.

'I am your great-aunt Annabelle—COME TO MIND YOU!' she grinned and fidgeted with her untidy pink shawl. She wore peculiar ancient looking clothes, and smelt of rainforest.

'We're going to get on splendidly!' she shouted. Piccolo, stunned, sincerely doubted it.

'Well? Am I going to grow old and die on the doorstep!?' she bellowed cheerily.

Piccolo thought, Suit yourself, but he gathered his manners and ushered her inside.

'I'd kill for a cuppa!' She flumped onto the ottoman, a big stuffed sofa.

'Please take a seat,' he murmured. 'I'll put the kettle on.'

Piccolo shuddered as Great-Aunt Annabelle, or whoever she was, slurped on dunked biscuits. She chattered away endlessly. Piccolo sat stonily, waiting for her to go away. He had important stamps to attend to.

'You are a quiet one, aren't you?' She sprayed soggy biscuit in Piccolo's direction. 'Would you have any fruit, my dear? Bananas perhaps? I've come a long way and . . .'

'My parents never mentioned that I had a great-aunt,' he interrupted stiffly, 'especially not a *flying* aunt.'

'Oh, I'm from a distant branch of the family tree,' she fidgeted. 'Did you call me a "flying" aunt! Ha ha ha! What a strange thing to say!' The great-aunt was clearly bothered.

'You are a fairy or something. I saw you fly into the pear tree,' said Piccolo flatly.

'Oh dear, you weren't supposed to see . . . how embarrassing . . . well . . . dear oh dear,' she burbled as she fished about in a floral bag. She found a little spray bottle and gave her face a few squirts.

'This is for stress. Very soothing. You try it.'

Before Piccolo could blink she sprayed him firmly in the face.

Piccolo spluttered, wiped his eyes, and said 'No, thank you!' too late.

'How was that? Do you feel better? A little sleepy maybe?' she enquired, watching him very closely.

'No. I feel damp, and you are not my aunt, great or ungreat!' Piccolo was losing his manners, his patience, and his temper.

'I'm sorry, dear. The spray usually works. Most odd,' said the strange woman. She continued, 'You are right, Piccolo dear. I'm not exactly

7

your great-aunt, although I'd be a very good one. You saw me flying, you say?'

'Yes. And not very well either.'

'Aha, yes! I'm a bit rusty, must admit. So you think I'm a fairy?' she asked as she busily sprayed more stress relief about the room, mostly towards Piccolo.

'An angel or a tooth fairy or something.

Would you please stop spraying me?' He sneezed.

Annabelle was watching him closely again.

'Are you sure you don't feel like a nap—forget all your troubles?' she asked.

'No,' said Piccolo firmly, 'and I don't have any troubles, or I didn't until very recently,' he added pointedly. The great-aunt seemed to make up her mind about something, then put the sprayer away.

'Well then, I am certainly *not* a fairy. I am an angel, Piccolo. I am your own personal Guardian Angel!'

She took a big breath and began talking in a rush.

'I'm not a perfect angel, to be honest. I'm a bit rough around the edges and my flying is hopeless, as you know. I can be a fumble bum and I can only cook fruit. I'm told I can talk a bit too much sometimes, and I get excited but . . .' she paused to take a big dramatic breath, '. . . I have a heart of gold.' She smiled sweetly and looked appealingly at Piccolo.

'I'd love to look after you. What do you say? Will you let me stay?' She breathed again and held it.

Piccolo sat and blinked at her. He was quite sure he did not need a guardian, especially not a noisy, foolish, round, feathered one. Life was orderly and comfortable in his lovely old home, if a little lonely at times. Very lonely, if he was honest. The peculiar being before him, still holding her breath, was turning crimson. It was very strange being asked for a job by an adult. Her eyes were watering now. He wondered if she might explode.

'I suppose you can stay, for a while,' he said at last 'just until . . .'

'OH JOY!' Annabelle exhaled explosively, and she lurched forward, smothering poor Piccolo in her bosom.

'You won't regret this, Piccolo my dear! We will have a wonderful time together!'

'I really like things quiet, you know,' he said, muffled in pinkness.

'Oh yes! I love the QUIET TOO!' said Annabelle, her voice rising happily.

CHAPTER TWO
Settling In

Four long days had passed since Piccolo had said,
'I suppose you can stay for a while, just until . . .'
He sat gloomily by the perch pond. From the
kitchen, Annabelle's cracked angel song rose
and fell through the back garden. The unhappy
boy sighed and wriggled his toes in the water.
The perch pond was his special place. This was
where he came when he needed to think. It
soothed and calmed him. He had been here
a lot lately, talking to his perch. It had been a
difficult few days. Not an hour had passed when

he did not ask himself why he had let her stay. The person was exhausting.

'Mum, Dad—she's quite mad.' The two perch nibbling his feet had taken the place of his dear missing parents. He had to complain to somebody. Piccolo was not normally a complaining sort of boy but these were unusual times.

'She *never* shuts up. She's broken half the crockery. She's always losing things. "Where's my shawl, Piccolo? Have you seen my bananas, Piccolo? Where's my brain, Piccolo?"' he mimicked unkindly. The perch looked up sympathetically as they nibbled a toe each.

'She's not my guardian; I'm hers! There's no peace, no quiet, I can't concentrate . . .'

Mum and Dad perch were wide-eyed with concern.

'She's like an enormous two year old, only sillier.'

He looked sternly into the water and said, 'She will have to go.'

13

Two days before, on the Monday morning, Piccolo had been very nervous as he left for school. He had written a long list of dos and don'ts for his visitor and stuck it to the fridge:

'Don't fly outside, don't make phone calls, do sit quietly and read, don't answer the doorbell.'

Annabelle had promised to be a perfect and obedient angel. She would sit in a comfortable corner and darn socks all day, she said.

But all day Piccolo wondered what he would find when he got home. Mrs Sweet, his teacher, noticed that her cleverest boy was distracted.

'Are you quite sure eleven times seven is "30 kilos of bananas", Piccolo?' There was much tittering as he looked at her blankly.

That afternoon he was hurrying along his driveway when he smelt smoke. 'Oh no!' he cried and he ran to the house. There was no fire. Instead he found Annabelle leaning over the sink, her hair caught in the plughole.

'It was just a little fire, and I put it out. And there's something wrong with the pasta-making thingy.' Piccolo stood in his kitchen and sighed. It looked as if badly behaved monkeys had been having a party. The curtains were singed, banana skins were everywhere, the pasta maker had a large tuft of wiry red hair poking out of it.

'I was making you some banana pasta. Ouch!' complained Annabelle as Piccolo cut her away from the plughole.

Piccolo did not go to school on Tuesday. He rang to say that he was having some 'family problems'. The problems continued on the Wednesday, Thursday, and, of course, Friday.

Annabelle had managed to start a drama or two daily. They came in all sizes and with great variety. There were the simple accidents; with taps, cutlery, and paper clips, for instance. And there were more serious mishaps. Early on Tuesday morning, for example, Annabelle had been 'taking her wings for a stretch' and become tangled in a tree by the driveway. She hung there trying to unknot her hair, calling 'Piccolo! Piccolo!' piteously. Young Henry the paper delivery boy stopped with his bicycle and gazed up at her.

'Oh hello, dear. Could you go to the house and find Piccolo, please? I'm a bit stuck.'

Henry found Piccolo in the vegetable patch in the back garden and handed him a newspaper.

'There's a pink lady stuck in a tree,' he said

gravely. 'She wants you to get her out.' He paused, 'Why has she got wings on?'

Piccolo dropped his rake and hurried to the driveway, then back to a shed for a ladder, an old mattress, and garden shears. Henry watched with interest as Piccolo snipped away at Annabelle's hair. She was nearly free when Henry said 'Bye. I have to deliver these papers,' and picked up his bike to go. Piccolo whispered to Annabelle, 'He's seen your wings. What if he tells someone?'

'Good thinking, my boy.' She called out, 'Don't go yet, dear! Stay a minute and have some fruit.'

'No thanks. Don't like fruit,' he called back.

'Strange child. He doesn't like fruit,' said Annabelle and she dropped to the mattress with a thud then half ran and half flew after Henry. She stopped him near the front gate. Piccolo watched her pull the small bottle from a pocket and spray him in the face. Henry swayed and dropped his bike. Annabelle caught him as his

Henry watched with interest.

legs folded, and laid him under a tree. Piccolo sprinted along the drive with her shawl.

'Quick, cover up! Someone else might see you!' Piccolo looked out of the gate left and right anxiously. He thought he spotted curious Mrs Jolly peering in their direction from her house on the corner.

'What did you do to him? You've knocked him out!' asked Piccolo as they carried him back to the house.

'Don't worry, Piccolo. I just gave him a quick squirt of my stress relief spray.'

'The stuff you sprayed me with? But it didn't put *me* in a coma.'

'He's not in a coma. He'll wake up in a minute, fresh as a daisy.'

They made him comfortable on the front verandah in a cane sofa with lots of cushions. Henry woke up twenty minutes later, as fresh as a limp lettuce, befuddled and confused.

'Where am I? Do you want a paper? I'll be late

for school,' he mumbled blearily.

'Hello, dear,' said Annabelle brightly. 'I'm Piccolo's great-aunt.'

She took his little limp hand and shook it. 'Would you like some fruit?' she added.

'Hello. I don't know.'

Later Henry, who had eaten his first pawpaw, wobbled off on his bicycle. Piccolo and Annabelle watched from the verandah.

'I think he's cured. He shouldn't remember anything about me and that wretched tree.'

'I hope so. Could you please not fly around any more, Annabelle. Some of the neighbours might not understand completely,' he sighed.

'What about the back garden? No one will see me there, my cautious boy. I need to keep fit, and lose a little weight,' she said, patting her very round hips. In the end Piccolo agreed that she could, in the back gardens, on moonless nights.

CHAPTER THREE
A Trip to the Shops

'And I'll never take her shopping again. That was *so embarrassing*!' Piccolo was by his special pond talking to Mum and Dad perch again.

He flushed all over at the memory. It had been a brave decision to take her out. They had run out of fruit. Annabelle wasn't happy with the quality that Piccolo was buying for her. She suggested that she might find some more to her liking.

'And you can't hide me in the house for ever, Piccolo.'

'I'm not hiding you,' he protested, realizing that he was doing just that.

'Then take me shopping. Please, Piccolo. I promise I'll behave myself.'

He agreed to take her that afternoon. Just a quick trip, to a little private greengrocer.

Piccolo normally caught the bus, but he decided that a taxi might attract less attention. Annabelle was nearly jumping out of her shawl with excitement as the taxi made its long way down the drive. It took Piccolo a very long time to put her seat belt on. She wriggled about, winding the window up and down, and flicking the ashtray lid.

'First time in a taxi, luv?' asked the observant driver.

'Yes! Isn't it wonderful?' Annabelle exclaimed.

'If you say so, luv,' said the weary man.

Annabelle behaved as if she had never been in any sort of vehicle. She grabbed Piccolo's arm as they accelerated down Pleasant Crescent, and gripped harder at every corner. The arm was going numb.

'Excuse me, sir? Is it necessary to go so very fast?' Sir assured her that they were only doing 43 kilometres per hour. After a while she relaxed her grip and began noticing things about her. She was constantly amazed by every ordinary thing.

'Look, Piccolo! Look at the size of that omnibus! Oh and look! That man has a tiny little dog! Hah! Have you ever seen such a fat cat in your life?' and so on and on until they arrived in the centre of town.

They needed fruit-buying money. Piccolo found the most out-of-the-way cash machine in Clearwater Bay. Annabelle yapped happily in the short queue about how sleek the carriages were these days and how much cleaner the streets were without horses. Again Piccolo wondered where she had been. A country with fruit and no cars—a tiny tropical island perhaps, with horses. When Piccolo's money appeared she went into noisy raptures.

'Free money! This is a land of miracles!'

Or maybe she's been locked in a cupboard for a hundred years, thought Piccolo.

By the time they reached Tony's Fruit and Vegetable Store, Piccolo was already exhausted. He had always shopped at Tony's, as his parents had before him. Annabelle took one quick look at his fruit displays and decided that Tony should sell up and try another business, and told him so.

'Look, Piccolo! There is an enormous shop over there. That must have better fruit!' and she headed in the direction of Buy-Plus. Piccolo apologized to the crestfallen Tony then had to stop Annabelle from stepping in front of a truck.

Inside Buy-Plus Piccolo tried out shopping trolleys until he found one that had four good wheels. Annabelle was sure she would need a trolley too for the amount of fruit they needed. She chose a squeaky one with a bad wheel. It pulled to one side. Two seconds into the pet food aisle Annabelle's wayward trolley clipped a carefully arranged tower of dog food tins. It teetered and collapsed as she continued unaware, sniffing the air. Following her nose, she squeaked her way to the fruit and vegetables, clipping everything on her left all the way. Poor Piccolo was left to chase about after cans, bottles, boxes, and tubes.

He found her sampling fruit and complaining loudly to a bewildered fruit and vegetable boy.

'Tasteless . . . green . . . Piccolo! Where have you been. This shop is disappointing, too, I'm afraid.'

He watched Annabelle as she poked and prodded, sniffed, bit, and bounced every example of fruit on display. She had a lot to say about each item, mostly negative, but still managed to fill her broken trolley. There were bananas, of course, pawpaw, mangoes, guavas, and strawberries, and a huge heavy watermelon on top of them all. Piccolo's trolley remained empty.

He found her sampling fruit, and complaining.

'Annabelle, will you stay here while I get a few things?' She was absolutely positive that she might, so Piccolo slipped quickly around to the dental care section. He tried to choose a floss.

'Mint, lemon grass, or plain? Um, um . . . waxed or unwaxed? . . . Quick! Choose!' He chose unwaxed mint, and was examining a toothbrush when he heard Annabelle's high voice in the distance.

She was arguing energetically with Sheryl, the checkout girl, insisting that since the fruit was no good it should be free. The store manager arrived and agreed strongly with Sheryl's point of view. Annabelle became heated and most unangelic.

'I'm leaving. Come on, Piccolo,' she huffed and pushed the trolley past the store authorities, banging her way out of the store. Piccolo tried desperately to explain and apologize, and to pay.

'She's been away a long time, on an island,

I think. It's her first time in a Buy-Plus . . .'

But the offended manager ignored him and called the police. Annabelle disappeared into the mall with her left-leaning load of stolen fruit.

Actually, the police had been very tolerant. They had not charged her with theft, cranky damage to property, or extreme rudeness to police officers. By the time Piccolo arrived Annabelle was calm and angelic. Sergeant McDouff was jotting down his mother's banana cake recipe for her. He even let her sound the siren on their way home. But for Piccolo, shopping with his aunt had been a major, serious embarrassment. In the back of the police car, slumped below window level, he vowed never to let her out of the house again. On the corner of Pleasant Crescent, inquisitive Mrs Jolly watered her driveway and peered disapprovingly into the car.

Back at the pond, the perch chewed Piccolo's

toes soothingly. They had to agree it had been an awful outing.

Piccolo wondered aloud. 'What am I going to do with her? How do you return a defective angel? Who do I complain to?' Mum and Dad perch seemed unsure what to suggest. But just as they were about to give some advice, perhaps, Annabelle yelled 'PICCOLO! Banana cake is ready!'

He sighed and trudged back to the house muttering to himself. 'I'll tell her now. She can't stay. "It's been an *interesting* time, but I'm really happier by myself", that's what I'll say.'

'It's a bit brown around the edges.' Annabelle did not need to explain. The kitchen was full of burnt banana fumes. The benches were strewn with skins and sticky blobs. Piccolo picked at the blackened edges of cake. He groaned to himself, or thought he had.

'Piccolo, I sense you're not completely happy,' said Annabelle with crumbs on her chin.

He was so unhappy that he could not look at her.

'Look, Annabelle, it's just that . . .' he began.

'I'm sorry I got a bit excited at the shops. They say it's my red hair . . . bit of a temper. You see, Piccolo . . .'

'A *bit* excited?' Piccolo bit his tongue, struggling to be the civilized boy his dear mother and father had brought him up to be. 'If you can't say anything nice about a person, it is probably best to say nothing at all' had been their advice. He picked away angrily at the burnt edges of his cake. There was almost none left.

'Well, yes, more than a bit excited. But that fruit, really . . . Anyway. You see, Piccolo, I've been away for a long time, and there's so much that's new and different here. I promise I'll try to be a cleverer great-aunt.' She reached out carefully with her chubby pink hand and held Piccolo's. 'But I'll need someone patient and wise to help me. Will you do that for me?'

Despite his very bad mood and disappointment with the cake, despite the speech he was trying to make, he felt a great warmth tingling through him from Annabelle's touch.

His anger slipped away. He sighed, exhausted by all these tiresome emotions, and ate a little of his dismantled cake. It was quite tasty after all. Maybe he *could* calm her down and civilize her a bit. Yes, I am a patient and wise boy, he thought agreeably, and a tidy and punctual one too. If there is anyone in Clearwater Bay who could tame this angel, it's me.

'Yes, I'll help you, Annabelle,' he heard

himself say. 'I'll help you be a normal great-aunt.'

'Wonderful! Let's celebrate; give ourselves a treat! How about a trip to the zoo?' she suggested brightly, squeezing his hand.

'The zoo . . . go out . . . to the zoo, with you? . . .' Piccolo looked at her doubtfully.

'I'll be the most ordinary aunt in the place,' promised Annabelle. 'I'll be quiet as a cucumber and as normal as a cup of tea. And you will be there to make sure I am.'

And so it was decided. Two hours after he had decided to tell her to leave, to go back to whatever strange place she had come from, they were going to the zoo instead.

CHAPTER FOUR
A Day at the Zoo

The next morning Piccolo rang the school again to say his family troubles were continuing, which was largely the truth. Annabelle was family of sorts, and she was trouble. He did not mention the zoo plan to Mrs Marshall, the school secretary, who was starting to worry about the boy. The boy was worried too. He was anxious about the upcoming outing, of course, and concerned about all the school he was missing. How, he wondered, would he ever catch up on his assignments, experiments, collections, projects,

research, revision, and homework. Even if he
tamed his great-aunt in just a few days, he would
be far behind. Thinking about it made him feel
worse. And Annabelle was not helping, bubbling
over with excitement, bobbing about the house
trying on different sunhats. To help himself calm
down Piccolo wrote a 'Zoo Outing' list of items
to pack in his sensible backpack. It read:
'sunscreen, water, camera, money, emergency
dried fruit, compass, matches . . .' Annabelle
presented herself for inspection.

'Introducing, for Piccolo, one unremarkable
and everyday great-aunt.' She twirled. The hat
was an enormous green straw thing adorned with
plastic grapes and figs. She had found a new
green shawl, as tatty as her old pink one, to
match the hat and hide her wings. Her dress was
all flounces and bows. Piccolo thought she
looked liked a mad tropical picture-book shep-
herdess. Annabelle thought she was the picture
of style and taste.

'Any last instructions, Piccolo dear, on being normal?'

'Just stay close to me, and try not to shout all the time,' he suggested.

'SHOUT? I DON'T SHOUT!' she shouted humorously.

Piccolo managed to get his great-aunt onto the bus without too much trouble. She had engaged in a loud conversation with the scruffy little dog that seemed to live at the bus stop.

'Hello my handsome little man,' she began.

'Arf, arf, yip, yip, arf woof!'

'Oh, yes I know, and we'd all better take care.'

'Yip, yip, growl, arrrrf arf!'

'A blessing, to be sure,' and other nonsense. No one in the queue had paid much attention, although some did step away a little. Once the bus arrived Piccolo led her all the way to the back seat, to be on the safe side. It was a jumpy walk down the aisle for Annabelle. She flinched at the driver, Mr Higgins, in his smart grey uniform, bustled quickly past old Mr Cox who always wore an ancient army coat and medals. She scowled at a little girl scout. When they reached the back of the bus, she flopped down with great relief.

'What is it about me and people in uniforms?' she wondered. 'Why do they always make me so nervous?'

She soon cheered up. This was only her third trip in a vehicle, after the taxi to the shops and the police car back home again. She pointed to this or that feature of the town, asking Piccolo what was what.

'That's the fire station. That's a bus stop. No, not ours, a different one. Ice skating rink. No, it's refrigerated. Yes, you've been there—the police station. The Town Hall. Yes, you could be mayor one day . . .' and so on.

All the while, a small girl stared at them from the seat in front. Piccolo studied a map of the zoo.

'Hello, darling. Are you going to the zoo? To see the chimps? I love the chimps best.' There was no answer, just more staring.

'Watch this, sweetie.'

Annabelle held up her hand, closed her eyes and strained until she went crimson. Piccolo looked up from his map. He was horrified to see that the chubby pink hand had lost its colour and had begun to go transparent. He grabbed it and hid it under his backpack.

'*Normal* great-aunt, remember!' he hissed.

'Yes of course, dear. Sorry. But did you see! I haven't done that for eons!'

The small girl was not impressed and turned her gaze to the bald man in front of her. She stared so hard at his shiny head that he had to put his hat on.

'*Normal,*' Piccolo hissed again.

'Yes, dear. Oh look! There's *another* bus! And here we are—the zoo!'

Piccolo's favourite part of the zoo was the Reptile House. He enjoyed the quiet calm of the fat blue-tongue lizards and the sleek elegance of the snakes. Annabelle, on the other hand, was hopping with boredom within a minute.

'Yes, Piccolo, that is a *beautiful* scaly-legged lump lizard. Um, would you mind much if I just popped over to the Primate Pavilion? Back in a minute!'

He thought, I shouldn't let her out of my sight, but he was half asleep gazing into the peaceful eyes of his lizard. An exciting new display—The Rare Desert Dozy Toad—caught his eye. Piccolo spent another six minutes admiring these sleepy creatures before he remembered his great-aunt.

'O-oh! She's probably inside a cage eating bananas by now.'

He was half right. Annabelle was eating fruit. Bananas were being poked through the cage for her by a family of happy chimpanzees. Between and during mouthfuls she chattered loudly with them, *in their own language.*

'Ooh-ooh-uh phppppptt ong,' observed a chimp.

'Oonga oonga eeepppffftt,' agreed Annabelle.

Piccolo had the Doctor Doolittle kind of fruity Guardian Angel apparently. At the very least she spoke Scruffy Dog and Chimp.

A medium-sized crowd of humans gathered, laughing quietly and shaking their heads. A few cameras whirred. Piccolo stepped back into the deep shadow of a tree and shuffled about, not knowing what to do. He hated a fuss, he avoided scenes. He considered running away and catching a bus home, and actually began to slide towards the exit. But when his great-aunt began to climb the bars crying 'Oo-oo-eee', Piccolo burst through the onlookers and tugged her down.

'Come on now, Annabelle. She's, um, not quite right . . .' he explained limply to the large crowd. They were disappointed as he bundled her away.

Piccolo stood very close to Annabelle in the queue at the Elephant and Beetle Café.

'You have to try harder, Annabelle. Normal great-aunts do not talk with chimps! Not in their own language, at least,' Piccolo whispered fiercely.

'Oh? Are you sure, dear?' said Annabelle doubtfully as she moved up to the counter.

'I'll have a banana split,' she said peering at

the blackboard menu '. . . but without the split.
Oh, and the Angel Cake!'

She half turned to Piccolo with a wink and a
big nudge, knocking the money out of his hand
in the process. Coins clattered, bounced, and
rolled in all directions, and a dozen people
chased them about. It was a busy minute before
Annabelle returned to the counter with most of
the money. Her hair was in extra disarray, her
shawl was hanging down, and one of her wings
was in full illegal view.

'Sorry, dear, where were we?' she asked the girl
behind the counter. 'What will you have, Piccolo?
Piccolo? There you are! What are you doing over
there?'

Piccolo emerged, bright red, from behind a
large potted palm, turned on his heel and left
the café.

'Goodness! What's bothering my boy, I
wonder? Not me I hope!' she chuckled bravely
at the sales girl.

They sat on a stone bench near the Unpopular and Ordinary Animal enclosure. Piccolo chewed slowly on his lunch. Annabelle had chosen him a banana and Vegemite sandwich. The boy was cross beyond speaking, or swallowing properly.

'Bengal tiger got your tongue, dear?' asked Annabelle after a while.

'Great-Aunt Annabelle,' he began icily. 'Your wing is showing.'

'Oh gracious . . . oh goodness! Did anybody see?' She flustered about rearranging her shawl to hide the brazen wing.

'No, not "anybody", just everybody in the café, and on that little train, and the tour group from Korea, and everyone else on the way here,' he said. 'I'm losing my famous patience, Annabelle, I really am.'

The brown Danish rat nearby sighed in his cage. People who came to sit at his corner of the zoo always had headaches or arguments or sore feet.

The boy was cross beyond speaking.

After his grumpy lunch, Piccolo's mood was not improved much by the hippos, the giraffes, and even another visit to the reptiles. But Annabelle was on her best behaviour. She politely admired a very dull lesser skink and sat quietly in the rear of the bus on the way home. Their outing had not been as wonderful as she had hoped. By and by Piccolo began to calm down. He would soon have his excitable guardian hidden safely away.

I'll lock her in the attic, no, the cellar, he smiled to himself, and poke bananas under the door every now and then. He chuckled at his unpleasant idea.

Annabelle thought the chuckle meant that she was being forgiven, and gave his hand a cautious little squeeze. Piccolo sighed. He was not an unpleasant boy, and he began to feel disappointed with himself for getting so angry. As he wondered if he should apologize, the bus stopped and a stern looking lady in uniform boarded. She moved slowly down the aisle. Annabelle became restless and fidgety as she came closer.

'What's she doing, Piccolo dear?' she whispered, clutching his arm.

'Looking at tickets. She's a Ticket Inspector,' said Piccolo.

'Inspector!' Annabelle breathed in sharply.

'It's OK, Annabelle. I've got ours here. See?' He held up their legitimate yellow tickets.

'Inspector . . . Inspection!' Annabelle seemed to be in a real panic.

'Really, Annabelle, it will be all right.' Piccolo was puzzled.

'No, Piccolo, you don't understand! What month is it today?'

'It's September today, and tomorrow, and . . .'

' "Sixteenth of September. Two thirty-five p.m. *sharp*",' she quoted. 'When is that?'

'About a week from now . . . six days,' he looked at his watch, 'and twenty-one hours and . . . eight minutes. Why, what's the matter?'

Before she could explain, their tickets were inspected, efficiently and humourlessly, and the bus arrived at their stop.

Annabelle collapsed onto the bench in the bus shelter.

'How could I forget! You are right, Piccolo! I am a silly old ninny,' she sighed.

'I never said that,' Piccolo objected. 'Not exactly.'

The bus stop dog was still there. He scrabbled out from under the bench and looked up at Annabelle. His little scruffy eyebrows were knotted with concern.

'I am a dope and a dupe and a dunce. You were quite correct, my clever Piccolo. I am a dunderhead and a dolt. Dear oh dear. What will I do?'

'About what?!' Piccolo was puzzled and a bit concerned by her sudden loss of self esteem.

'An Inspector of Guardian Angels is coming to inspect me, on the sixteenth of September. I completely forgot. I've been so happy and excited lately . . .' She sighed again. 'That's why uniforms are bothering me. Angel Inspectors always wear uniforms, and I don't like Angel Inspectors one bit. When you called that sour old ticket woman an "Inspector" it all came rushing back.'

'What are they going to inspect?'

'Me. You see, I am on probation—I'm sort of on angel P-plates. And some of my skills are, um, a bit rusty. Very rusty. I should have been practising and practising every spare moment.'

'And if you fail, what will happen?' asked Piccolo, carefully.

'I'll be sent far away, back to where I came from, I expect.'

Piccolo thought about this. Annabelle looked sideways at him. 'You might be thinking "Yay!" to that . . . but I would miss you terribly.'

Piccolo looked at his shoes a little guiltily. Yesterday he would have said 'Yay'. Two hours ago, after the scene with the chimpanzees, he would have said 'Yippidy Yay!' But now she looked so miserable in her great silly hat . . .

Annabelle banged her head softly against the back of the bus shelter. 'A dolt I am.'—thud—'A dim-witted, dopey dunce,'—thud—'floundering, forgetful fool,' she muttered.

While Annabelle thudded, Piccolo thought. I was happy on my own, except for missing my parents. I miss my quiet life; my stamps, my own cooking. And I'm embarrassed to death every time we leave the house. But then again . . .

'Ninny, nurdle'—thud—'nitwit, no brain'—thud—continued Annabelle. The scruffy dog was sitting on the bench with a paw on her lap and his head to one side.

'Arf, yip?' it asked.

'Yower yip yip woof,' explained Annabelle.

Glancing at her round miserable face,

Piccolo noticed her eyes properly for the first time. He had always thought they were piggy and squinty. Instead he was surprised to see round eyes of the clearest blue. Annabelle looked directly at him. For a moment he was lost in them, in two pools of sweetness so pure that he had to blink and look away. Whether it was those eyes or his own good nature he was not sure, but he said, 'I'll help you get ready for the Inspection, Annabelle.'

'You will? Oh, you wonderful boy!' she choked, and as the little dog yapped happily, Piccolo braced himself for another great pink smothering.

CHAPTER FIVE
Angel in Training

The next morning, bright and early, Piccolo sat down at his dear missing mother's writing desk. He had a sharp pencil, an accurate set square, and several crisp sheets of white paper. A pencil sharpener sat at the ready nearby.

'Annabelle, we need a list. My father always said, "Lists are the cornerstone of civilization—along with cold showers on Sundays and prune juice in the morning". Now, what sorts of things will be tested?'

Annabelle was flumped on the ottoman, her

hair aflame and askew. She was a perfect picture of untidy uncertainty.

'Oh goodness, how does it go?' she sighed. 'It's been such a very long time since I've had one.'

'What about hair care?' suggested Piccolo cheekily. List-making always improved his humour.

'Yes, hair care is one,' agreed Annabelle seriously. 'They test angel things and ordinary things. Why? What's wrong with my hair?' she asked, tugging at a tangled lock.

'What about flying?' Piccolo changed the subject.

'Yes, and there is Transformation, where you turn yourself into other people or things. Heavenly Song,' she went on. 'You've heard me sing, Piccolo. Do I sound heavenly? A little practice perhaps?'

'Just a little,' agreed Piccolo, spreading his arms out wide.

'No need to be rude, dear,' she said. 'Now let me think . . . What else? Of course! Mystification.'

'Is that "M-i-s" or "M-y-s"?' asked Piccolo as he added it to his list. 'And what does it mean?'

'It's "M-y-s" like in "mystery" and it's to help people forget. Remember when poor Henry saw me in, um, difficulties in that blessed tree?'

'You knocked him out with your stress relief spray,' remembered Piccolo.

'Yes, I had to. If a human sees too much angel stuff, like flying or transforming or going invisible, it makes them forget. It Mystifies them.'

'But it didn't work on me. And you nearly drowned me in the stuff.'

'That's right, and that is a mystery and a secret,' she was quite serious now, and dropped her voice to a whisper, 'especially when the Inspector comes. He mustn't guess that I couldn't Mystify you, or that you know I'm not your great-aunt.'

'Maybe I'm part angel,' Piccolo joked.

'Or an Angelspotter is my guess,' said Annabelle.

'An Angelspotter? The only angel I've ever spotted was you.'

'Maybe so,' said Annabelle, 'but you are immune to Mystification, which means you are an Angelspotter, unless there's something wrong with my formula.'

'It worked fine on Henry,' chuckled Piccolo. 'Anyway, why is it such a big secret?'

'Two reasons,' Annabelle began. 'First, if an Angel Authority, like my Inspector for instance, finds out, you'll be taken away. They'll put you in a special school for young Angelspotters.'

'What? Whether I want to go or not?' asked Piccolo alarmed.

'I'm afraid so. And the second, much less important reason, is that I will be punished for keeping your special talent a secret.'

'The Angel Authorities sound very strict.'

'Yes they are. All rules and ironed uniforms, perfect hair and teeth. So make another list, Piccolo. Call it "Piccolo's Rules to Avoid Detection".'

This was not the list they were supposed to be working on, but Piccolo couldn't resist a list, however strange. He wrote as Annabelle dictated.

'One: Never tell *anyone,* ever, that your great-aunt is a Guardian Angel.

Two: Especially people in uniforms. They could be Angel Authorities.

Three: If sprayed by anyone for any reason by anything, pretend to be Mystified. It might be an angel trying to Mystify you.'

'What about Mrs Jolly on the corner? She's always spraying everything with her garden hose. Is she an angel?'

'Possibly. I don't know all of them, of course.'

Annabelle dictated a sublist (Piccolo especially loved sublists): 'Symptoms of Mystification'

- confusion and drowsy grogginess, followed by
- sleep, followed by
- complete forgetfulness.

Annabelle insisted that Piccolo practise looking Mystified. She produced her 'stress relief' spray and squirted him. Feeling foolish at first, Piccolo acted out the sublist. He wobbled about blinking heavily and bumping into furniture, fell onto the

ottoman, snored loudly, bounced up and said, 'Hello. Who are you and what's for lunch?' Piccolo had not been so silly since his parents went missing, and he felt better for it.

But Annabelle frowned. 'That was *good*—but a bit too much. This is serious. Being an Angelspotter is a big secret to keep.'

It was morning tea time already. Annabelle's Inspection list was still very sketchy. So after some quick banana biscuits and a fruit tea he marched Annabelle back to the ottoman. In half an hour they had a satisfactory list. It read:

<u>Inspection Subjects</u>
a. Angel Items
Invisibility, Flying, Transformation, Mystification, Angel Lore and Law, Harp Playing, Heavenly Singing
b. Earthly Items
cooking, personal grooming, household care, general knowledge, earthly singing

Beneath this he had drawn up a timetable for each hour of each day up until the Inspection.

He read it out again. Annabelle nodded heartily.

'That is a serious and fine list and schedule. Thank you, Piccolo. Now what say we go to the shops for some helpful magazines with ten minute meals and hair advice?'

'Annabelle, no. If you will look at your copy of the timetable it says Flying 10.30 to 11.05. It is 10.25 now, so let's get started.'

'Yes, I suppose we must,' sighed Annabelle as she uncurled herself from the ottoman.

'Yes, we must.' Lists brought out a happy bossy side of Piccolo's personality. He had to admit it was good to have someone to boss about.

The Flying lesson proved to be more complicated than Piccolo had imagined. It had to be held indoors, of course, to avoid detection. The ballroom was a good size but Annabelle was very rusty indeed. By 10.35 the fine crystal chandelier was a pile of fine crystal bits on the fine marble floor. The huge oil painting of Grandpa was skewered on a precious lamp by 10.36. Piccolo moved 'accuracy' above 'speed & altitude' on the 'Flying Priorities' sublist. The rest of the lesson was spent removing valuables and assembling mattresses, cushions, and egg cartons around the room.

After Heavenly Singing, Piccolo needed a quiet time with a cold pack on his head, which reduced Invisibility lesson time to twenty minutes. Annabelle managed a transparent foot, but then she had a headache of her own from the strain.

Mystification was less trouble at first, being more like cooking. Annabelle fetched little secret bags of herbs from her floral bags. Soon a fresh brew of stress relief spray bubbled on the stove. Pungent fumes filled the house and drifted outside. Cockroaches and little lizards staggered about. In a separate saucepan she experimented with a double strength batch with extra-secret ingredients.

When it had cooled, Annabelle asked, 'Can I just try something on you, dear?' and before he had time to say 'What?' she sprayed the poor boy full in the face.

'Annabelle! You know I'm immune! Yuck!' he protested. Once again nothing happened, apart from a runny nose and stinging eyes.

'You're a tough little angelspotting fellow, Piccolo. That was a rare and ultra-secret super-brew.' Annabelle was more convinced than ever that her boy was an extra-special one. She put the failed experiment in her pocket.

'I still need something sizeable to try my regular brew on. Something big in a uniform perhaps. The postman?'

'No, Annabelle. Don't even think about it. Things would get complicated for sure. What about Rex?' he suggested. 'It's nearly twelve thirty. He will be passing by soon.'

Rex was a dopey local Alsatian dog that wandered past their gate every morning on his way to water Mrs Jolly's hibiscus bush.

Annabelle and Piccolo hurried up the long gravel driveway to lay an ambush.

'Here he comes!' whispered Piccolo as they crouched behind the gateposts.

'Here, boy! Here, Rex!' Rex was as deaf as he was dopey and failed to notice them. He shuffled past the gate and on his way to his appointment with the bush.

'Oh botheration,' said Annabelle. She quickly looked up and down Pleasant Crescent, stepped out onto the street and squirted poor old Rex. He dropped like a rock. Annabelle stood over him for a moment to make sure the poor old thing was still breathing.

'Excellent,' she said, grinning at Piccolo.

'Annabelle! Someone could be watching you!'

Indeed, someone was. Mrs Jolly witnessed this odd little scene from her front garden. She felt cheated. She had been waiting for Rex with her garden hose.

They left Rex next to the driveway to sleep it off and returned to the house. Annabelle was still not satisfied.

'A dopey old dog is all well and good, but a human guinea pig would be so much better,' she mused.

'Annabelle! Really! No,' Piccolo warned again.

Unhappily, as it would turn out, a human guinea pig appeared later that morning. Piccolo was in the attic at the time, looking for his mother's old harp. Kevin the Expensive Fruit delivery man arrived with specially imported fruit. Annabelle had ordered it by telephone. She had a puzzling fondness for African fruit. She opened the door and flinched at the khaki uniform with pineapple badges.

'Just leave it there on the step, thank you,' she said quickly. Then suddenly she thought 'Guinea Pig' and asked him to bring them into the kitchen instead. Kevin put the big baskets on the kitchen table.

'Lovely, lovely. Ooh! Look at those red bananas!' exclaimed Annabelle, slowly reaching for her spray.

'Little beauties, aren't they. And look at the size of the Oomgarbbi nuts!' said Kevin with pride. Annabelle thought of a way to make a test more believable.

'I'm so impressed with this bounty, I could flap for joy! Oh, for heaven's sake, look! I am!'

Kevin watched, stupefied, as Annabelle unfurled her wings and flew clumsily around the kitchen table, singing:

Fruit, fruit, glorious fruit,
the more you eat, the more you hoot,
Fruit's a hoot . . . oops.'

She spotted Piccolo standing at the kitchen door and landed with a thud.

'Oh, hello dear. I was just thanking Kevin for the fruit,' she grinned guiltily. Piccolo glared at her, but it was too late to cancel the experiment.

Kevin watched, stupefied.

'Thanks again, Kevin, and goodnight.' She sprayed the poor gaping man, who dropped like a tree trunk.

'Wow,' said Annabelle, a bit taken aback. 'That worked quickly.'

Piccolo took the bottle. 'Because you used the wrong spray! This is the extra strong stuff you tried on me!' He was flapping his own arms with frustration. 'I told you not to even think about it. I'll have to call an ambulance! We could go to jail for this!'

'Don't be dramatic, dear. He'll be fine. I'll just cook up an antidote.'

But Piccolo refused to let her try, in case she killed him completely. He sat anxiously near Kevin listening to his breathing. The big man did not wake after twenty minutes, like little Henry the paper boy. At midnight he was still snoring. They tried a bucket of ice water on his head. This made no impression at all, so they dragged him by the ankles along the hallway, down the front steps and, with difficulty, back up again. This failed too. Annabelle sang, which would normally wake a brick post, but Kevin slumbered on. At two in the morning they gave up and took turns to watch him through the rest of the night.

Piccolo was dozing when Kevin woke with a jolt at nine o'clock.

'Ow. I've banged my head. Is the fruit all right? Goodness! Is that the time. I'm running early,' and shuffled in a dazed hurry to his van and drove away.

'I suppose he'll notice that it's not yesterday by and by. Oh well, never mind,' said Annabelle philosophically.

'At least he's not dead,' said Piccolo, but he was not as relaxed as his great-aunt. This was a boy who knew the importance of lists and timetables. When Kevin was properly awake he would surely wonder about his missing day.

CHAPTER SIX
A Transformation

It was time for the Transformation lesson. Piccolo chose a photo of a short round gentleman in a suit as reference. Not a long thin man in shining armour, or an elaborate lamp-post, but something simple, they thought. Annabelle had strained and grunted and strained well into Angel Lore revision time. She had transformed, eventually, into a beach ball shaped thing with flaming red hair.

'It will wear off soon,' the ball squeaked.

There was a knock at the door.

'Don't move, Annabelle,' Piccolo warned, as he wedged her under a chair. Standing on his toes he peered through the spy hole at the front door. He saw a spherical grinning woman and, behind her, a tall young man with a camera.

'Where the blazes *are* they?' the woman grimaced impatiently, as she turned the handle and shoved hard on the door, catching poor Piccolo's nose on the other side.

'Ow!'

'Piccolo Grande!' cried the intruder with half her pointy head and a foot in the hallway. 'Do you remember me? Erica Stringer from the *Clearwater Klaxon*, and this is Todd. We did a story on you when your parents died?'

'They're not dead,' corrected Piccolo indignantly, his hand on his nose, and his shoulder against the door. 'They are just missing.' Piccolo remembered Erica Stringer. He did not like her then and he was not liking her again now.

'Yes, of course they are, darrrling. And you be

sure to call me the second they're found. We'll do a big colour supplement in the Sunday paper about their adventures.'

'What do you want?' said Piccolo. He strained against the door with all his small weight and managed to wedge an umbrella under it. They absolutely could not come inside, because of the thing under the ballroom chair.

'Oh, we just wanted to follow up, see how you're doing,' she grinned, her eyes darting about the hallway, probing. This was not the real reason for her visit. Miss Stringer had information.

As Piccolo had feared, Kevin the Expensive Fruit man did notice that he had lost a day. Going back through his delivery list, he figured that the old Grande place was involved but he had no memory of being there at all. He told his strange tale to a customer; Henry the paperboy's mother. Henry had told her a very similar tale, and she told both stories to her sister, June, who worked at the *Clearwater Klaxon.* June told Miss Erica Stringer. And here she was, pushing on the door and swivelling her turtle neck about Piccolo's hall. Clearwater Bay was a small town and news travelled quickly.

A popping sound and a squeal came from the direction of the ballroom. Todd's head joined Miss Stringer's at the door. Piccolo turned to see what the noise was, and all three of them watched as Annabelle rolled slowly from the ballroom into the hall, bounced gently off the wall opposite and rolled back into the ballroom.

Zzzrrrpp zzzrrrp zzzrrrpp went Todd's camera.

'What was that! Did you get it, Todd? Tell me you got it!' cried Miss Stringer. Piccolo struggled to shut the door but heads and a camera were blocking it. He stamped as hard as possible on a pointy foot. The intruders recoiled. Piccolo slammed the door and locked it and ran to the ballroom.

'I'm sorry, Piccolo,' squeaked Annabelle.

Piccolo turned to see what the noise was.

'It was uncomfortable under the chair. I just wriggled a bit and accidentally popped out and . . . Did they see me?' Piccolo looked past her. A camera was appearing and disappearing at one of the windows. Todd was jumping up and down snapping. Piccolo ran over and pulled the curtains.

'Yes, they did,' he called as he ran to lock all the windows and doors.

He returned breathless.

'Piccolo, it might be safest if you Mystified them. I would, but . . .' squeaked the beach ball.

'But how!' Piccolo collapsed on a chair. 'It's hopeless. I'm locked in here and they're prowling outside. Are you at least trying to, you know, de-ball?' He was irritable. His nose hurt.

'Of course I am. I'm nearly popping with the effort. But listen, Piccolo. You're a clever boy. Think of a way to ambush them with my spray. I'm not sure if it will work for you, not being an angel, but it's worth a try. I can't have my photo in the paper, not looking like this.'

'All right, I'll try.' Piccolo stood up wearily and took the bottle.

Soon he was wriggling out of a cellar window and creeping, doubled over, through the olive trees. He reached the Klaxon car and crouched behind it. Miss Stringer was on Todd's high shoulders trying to climb onto the verandah roof.

I forgot the upstairs windows! thought Piccolo. I'll have to spray them before they get in the house.

He hesitated. How on earth was he going to tackle two ambitious and determined adults? As he fretted, Todd staggered and Miss Stringer tumbled into a rose bush. Todd thought about running away at this point, being rather terrified of the scrawny reporter. But he carefully helped his boss out of the flower bed. She was thoroughly scratched and irate. Todd was belted with a microphone for his troubles.

'I give up!' she yelled. 'For now!' and turned to the car.

Piccolo quickly opened a back door and hid. He had read about this strategy any number of times. To succeed with the hiding-in-the-back-of-the-car plan, he needed material to hide under. For this Piccolo found a jumbo pizza box, plenty of old newspapers, several drink cans, and dozens of chocolate bar wrappers. Newspaper people are certainly pigs, thought Piccolo as he quickly buried himself.

Also, for the plan to work, the car owners needed to both sit in the front and to be very unobservant. Piccolo would need to not sneeze, cough, or burp. He held his breath as Todd opened a door to throw in his camera bag unobservantly then fold himself into the driver's seat. Miss Stringer was too busy bleeding to notice the swollen pile of rubbish behind her.

Piccolo's plan had worked well so far, but it still had many weak points. If he just popped up and sprayed, for instance, there could be a terrible accident. Todd, the driver, might leap with fright and lose control of the vehicle. Or the spray might not work at all. His enemies would just be damp and extremely curious. Or he could stay hidden, slowly fill the car with spray from his hiding place and see if it worked. If it did, he could only hope that the car might roll to a gentle stop. He decided to try plan B, and sooner rather than later, before they left quiet Pleasant Crescent for the busy streets of town. The crunching of the gravel driveway drowned out the rustle of rubbish as Piccolo got Annabelle's little bottle out of his pocket. Poking the nozzle up through his camouflage he began to spray. Todd had just turned the car out onto the street, and had time to say, 'What's that smell?'

Miss Stringer just had time to reply, 'What sm—' before Todd's foot slipped off the accelerator. The car rolled gently to a stop. Piccolo peeked out of his hiding place.

Perfect! The extremely risky plan B had worked. The car had veered harmlessly onto a grassy verge, and his enemies were Mystified. Piccolo admired his handiwork. He pinched Miss Stringer's stringy neck to check that she was sound asleep, and once again, harder than necessary, to make absolutely sure. He pocketed the precious spray bottle and opened a back door to make his way home. Suddenly he remembered Todd's camerawork. There were three cameras in two bags and a dozen rolls of film lying about the back seat. To be on the safe side he emptied all the cameras, pocketed the films and all the loose rolls as well. He stepped cautiously out of the car into a flower bed.

'O-oh. Mrs Jolly's jonquils.' As casually as he could manage Piccolo looked towards the house, and there was Mrs Jolly peering through the curtains, and dialling on her telephone. Piccolo waved nonchalantly and walked casually, then quickly, home. He wondered how much she had seen, and if she was ringing the police, and whether he should be spraying her too. He would enjoy that, spraying unpleasant Mrs Jolly, but he might need to spray poor Mr Jolly as well, and their cat Flossie, and eventually the whole street.

Piccolo knocked on his front door.

'Who's there?' Annabelle squeaked.

'It's me. They've gone.'

'Gone? Just a minute . . . I can't reach the

handle . . . I'll try to get a bit of a bounce going . . .'

Piccolo stood patiently, listening to thump, squeak, thump, squeak until Annabelle managed to snare the lock first and, on another bounce, the handle. She was more her old self again, more of a sausage shape now than a beach ball. She was bouncing with worry. Piccolo told her of his triumph in the Klaxon car. Annabelle ballooned about with congratulations.

'At the last minute I remembered Todd's photos,' he said emptying out a dozen rolls of film onto the table.

'Oh, you clever, clever, clear-headed darling. I never would have thought of that.'

Piccolo smiled at the praise, then remembered Mrs Jolly spying.

'Don't you worry about that nosy old thing!' said Annabelle breezily. She was not going to let little complications spoil their victory.

That was the end of lessons for the day.

Piccolo spent the rest of the afternoon attaching a huge noisy cow bell to the front gate. From now on the gate would stay closed.

Piccolo needed to settle down after the day's drama. He treated himself to a brand new HB pencil from his stationery cupboard under the stairs and a fresh sheet of paper. Sitting at his mother's desk he settled down to rewrite tomorrow's timetable. This was much more his cup of hot chocolate than squirting adults in a moving vehicle.

Meanwhile, on the kitchen floor downstairs, Annabelle grunted and strained as she tried to transform back to her old self. Exhausted, she eventually gave up and wriggled off to bed looking like a fat sausage with flippers for arms and legs.

'Annabelle old girl,' she said to herself as she squirmed along the hall, 'you are embarrassing yourself, and that isn't an easy thing to do.'

CHAPTER SEVEN
A Fully Trained Angel

The next morning Annabelle was her old self with a full set of working limbs. Piccolo sat her down firmly and they began working their way through the new timetable. Yesterday's dishes were still in the sink, joined by a couple of hasty breakfast bowls. Annabelle noticed that Piccolo was not wearing a tie.

Bless the boy, she thought, for me he has gone tieless.

General knowledge was first.

Her general knowledge was generally missing.

Piccolo soon put away the books from his father's beautiful twenty-four volume encyclopaedia. They were now using Piccolo's old *Big Book of Fun Facts for Little Folk*.

'Who is the queen of Australia?' he asked. 'No, that's too hard.' He tried again. 'When was the first moon landing?'

'Oh! I know this one! It was the Angel Azekial, two and a half million years ago, roughly.'

Annabelle beamed with pride. This was the first one she felt sure about.

'Well, I actually meant "When was the first *human* moon landing?"' Piccolo corrected.

'This is a trick question, isn't it, quiz master Piccolo? People can't go to the moon!' she said with a sly twinkle.

'Never mind.' He flipped to another page. 'Let's see . . . Name three kinds of tropical fruits.'

'The Umbamatto, Green Squahilla, and Livingstone beans,' she answered rapidly and confidently.

These were not listed in the *Book of Fun Facts* with pineapple and mango, so he went back to the encyclopaedia to check.

'Believe me, I know my fruit, Piccolo. Especially African, equatorial. Very green, and warm there . . . friendly faces . . . I do miss them . . .' Annabelle trailed off, remembering.

Remembering what, Piccolo wondered as he flicked pages. Yes, they were all there.

'Well,' he said, impressed. 'Let's hope you get a lot of questions about tropical, African, jungle fruit.'

Invisibility was next on the timetable. Annabelle made herself comfortable on the ottoman and closed her eyes. After fifteen minutes of straining and grunting she was still perfectly, scruffily visible. Annabelle sank back into the cushions breathing heavily.

'I did better in the bus. Does that big toe look a bit translucent to you, Piccolo?' she asked hopefully. He couldn't tell.

'Does it always take so much effort, Annabelle?'

'Oh no,' she sighed. 'I used to be able to blink on and off like a light switch. I'm just a wee bit rusty but I'll get the knack back.'

'It looks very difficult. Perhaps, if you sort of relaxed and concentrated . . .' he suggested.

But Annabelle was already red-faced and cross-eyed again. Piccolo heard a distant musical clunking, like a big bell.

'The front gate!' he yelped, remembering his cow bell installation. He left Annabelle straining on the ottoman and hurried about locking all the doors and windows. It could be the horrible Ms Stringer again. A vehicle crunched along on the gravel driveway. Piccolo watched from behind a curtain. It wasn't the Klaxon car. This one had blue stripes and lights on top and big black letters along the side.

'The police? What do they want?' wondered Piccolo. 'Oh no! . . . Mrs Jolly?' She had watched him step onto her jonquils.

Piccolo thought about hiding in his stationery cupboard under the stairs. But Annabelle might answer the door, half invisible.

'Good morning, Piccolo. Sergeant McDouff, Clearwater Police. You remember, we met when your aunt, ah, went shopping . . .'

Of course Piccolo remembered, painfully well.

'I'd like to have a few words with you if I may.'

Piccolo led Sergeant McDouff into the kitchen and sat him down. He fussed about making tea, cutting banana cake, and chatting aimlessly. The whole time he struggled to think of a story to explain the car in Mrs Jolly's jonquils. Sergeant McDouff had finished a second cup of tea and a fourth piece of cake, and Piccolo had still not thought of anything.

'No thanks, no more cake, son. Diet,' he explained poking his generous tummy. 'So . . . so,' he began in his flat policeman's tone, and flipping open his notebook, 'yesterday, about noon, a Clearwater Klaxon's car was observed with the motor running on Mrs Jolly's front garden. Two employees of the newspaper, Ms Stringer and her photographer, Todd, were found unconscious in the vehicle. As of this morning they remain in a state of confusion and cannot account for their being there. Can you explain what you were doing at the scene, Master Grande?'

'Ah, well, they came here first . . .' Piccolo began in a high strangled voice. He felt a sweaty kind of drowning feeling under the bland gaze of the detective. This man had listened to a

thousand liars, and could see through the best of them. Piccolo, a serious and honest boy, had never told a lie in his life.

'. . . and tried to come inside. I didn't ask them in. I don't like them very much.'

'I'm with you there, son,' the sergeant mumbled quietly. 'Nosy, desperate types . . .'

'Anyway, they came to the door . . .' Piccolo's head began to swim with the effort of dishonesty, 'and I wouldn't let them in . . .'

'So you said,' said the sergeant.

'They took you for a drive, didn't they, my dear?' said Annabelle appearing suddenly. 'Hello, Jim! That's your recipe you're eating there. Do you remember me? I was at your prison place?'

The policeman said he would never forget, and smiled at the memory.

'Yes, they took you for a drive. Didn't they say that they had a lead on your poor missing parents, Piccolo?'

'Ah, yes, I think so. Something like that.'

'"Something like that . . ."' muttered Sergeant McDouff as he wrote Piccolo Grande's first lie down in a police notebook.

'They wanted you to look at a life vest they'd found, was it?' continued Annabelle, lying fluently. 'But the poor things were so exhausted from the high paced newspaper life. They nodded off, didn't they, Piccolo, before they'd left Pleasant Crescent.'

'Yes, it was a short drive.' This was true, Piccolo thought. It had been a very short drive, thanks to him.

'It was a blessing that no one was hurt. You weren't hurt were you, dear?'

'No, no. I was fine . . . luckily,' said honest Piccolo.

'I wanted to report them for dopey driving, but Piccolo felt sorry for them. That's the kind-hearted boy he is, Jim—much like yourself.'

Sergeant Jim wrote 'much like myself' carefully in his notebook.

'Ms Stringer was covered in scratches and several rose thorns were found embedded in her. That sort of thing would keep a person wide awake, don't you think, Piccolo?'

'I, um, yes I suppose so . . .' Piccolo was drowning again.

'Shock,' said Annabelle. 'Shock, Jim. She'd fallen in the rose bush, and must have fallen asleep with the shock and loss of blood, poor skinny thing. Not enough blood in her.'

'Yes, she lost a lot of blood,' Piccolo exaggerated, with a supreme effort. He studied the floor, hiding his discomfort, and felt the policeman's gaze boring into the top of his head. He could see his own unhappy face in his shoes, which were polished as always to a mirror shine. Sergeant McDouff's big boots could do with a bit of work, he thought, and Annabelle had never cleaned her shoes in her life. He glanced over at her scruffy pink footwear, but they were missing—invisible, along with her feet!

McDouff carried on, unaware of the discovery.

'Doesn't explain their loss of memory, or the loss of all the photographer's film though,' he said.

'Stress I'd say, Jim, causing them to fall asleep and lose things,' Annabelle suggested.

'Yes. Well, I expect you're right.' He closed his notebook. 'There are a lot of odd things happening around town lately. Around Pleasant Crescent to be more specific.' He shifted his heavy gaze from Annabelle to Piccolo and back again. 'Number 9 to be particularly specific.' Piccolo wriggled uncomfortably, but Annabelle just smiled, bright and innocent.

'Why that's our place, Jim! Fancy that! What sort of things?'

'Oh, just little things, like the Klaxon incident, and you hear tales in my line of work, about paper boys and delivery men . . .' He gazed slowly at Piccolo, then at Annabelle.

'Where did you say you were from again, Miss Grande?' he asked pleasantly.

'You remember, Jim. I told you before,' she said with her sweetest smile. Piccolo froze as he watched her carefully place her antique spray bottle on the table. Stress relief!

Don't you dare! he screamed silently.

'You said something about the fruit being better in Africa. Where precisely in Africa are you from?' the sergeant probed.

Annabelle picked up the bottle and said vaguely, 'Oh, it's such a big place, Jim . . .' She gave herself a quick squirt. 'There was a river, I remember, big and brown. The Congo, I think . . .' She moved the bottle casually in the sergeant's direction.

Piccolo was about to make a grab for it, or fall off his chair, or choke loudly on a passing fly, he hadn't decided, when the big policeman stood up and said, 'Well that's interesting, but I'd better get back to detecting. Thanks for the tea, Piccolo, and the cake, Miss Grande.'

When the detecting sergeant left, with the last

of the cake, Piccolo and Annabelle flopped onto the ottoman.

'Were you seriously going to Mystify him?' said the exhausted boy.

'It crossed my mind. He is a sweetie, my big Jim, but he was getting a bit close and personal there.'

'I hate lying,' breathed Piccolo. 'You are good at it though. Are all angels such good liars?'

'That wasn't lying, dear. That was careful tale-telling to protect the innocent.'

'Well, I hope it worked. And it's a good thing he didn't detect your feet, Annabelle.'

'My feet?' She looked where they would normally be, small and dainty at the end of her legs.

'Hooray! No feet! The knack's coming back!' and she danced a little foot-free jig to celebrate.

When Annabelle had calmed down, Piccolo looked at the timetable.

'We're running very late for Angel Lore and Law,' he announced. 'What can I do to help?'

'I'll have to study this alone, I'm afraid, dear. There is a Book, and mortals, even clever and honest ones like you, cannot look at it. It's a rule.'

Piccolo was curious, being a book-loving boy.

'But you're not exactly *strict* with the rules . . .'

'Well, yes, there are a lot of silly rules, I think, but they'd have my wings if I broke this one. There are things in there that would be harmful for you to see. So I'll just pop up to my room and give it a quick run through.'

Piccolo was now very curious. He tried to settle into refreshing the timetable, but he couldn't concentrate. There was a secret Book upstairs in Annabelle's room. After sharpening his pencil, then a box of pencils, and emptying the shavings and ruling some lines, he couldn't stand it any more. He crept up the stairs.

A golden glow shone out from under Annabelle's door. Piccolo knocked softly. The door swung open a little. He peeked inside. Annabelle was snoozing, her head on the table. Next to her was a glowing book. The boy, not a sneak by nature, sneaked awkwardly across the room.

It was an enormous book. He held his breath and peered through and around Annabelle's hair. The little he could see was entrancing. Golden swirling lettering seemed to shift on the page. There were tiny, intensely detailed illustrations, pulsing with energy. In a kind of trance, Piccolo reached out to touch the book. Annabelle, snoring softly all the while, suddenly snorted loudly, said 'Beware', then began snoring again. Piccolo froze, his heart stuck guiltily in his throat, and tiptoed swiftly out of the room.

Piccolo spent the next hour wondering whether he had been caught out or not. He paced about, did the dishes, put on a tie, ironed some socks.

At last Annabelle came downstairs, humming tunelessly.

Piccolo hoped that was a good sign.

'Ah, time well spent. I feel much brainier, and I think I had a nap,' she said plainly. 'What's next? I'm ready for anything.'

Piccolo looked at the timetable, much relieved. His sneaking had been undetected, it seemed.

'Personal grooming. Perhaps we could start with your hair?'

This was far less fascinating than the Book, thought Piccolo. But the need for tidiness was strong in him. He had been itching to work on Annabelle's blackberry patch for ages.

'My hair? What's wrong with it?' Annabelle was puzzled. Hers was a magnificent, interesting, energetic head of hair.

'Nothing,' lied Piccolo quickly. 'It's just there might be a split end or two, and I think I saw something moving in there.'

So Annabelle sat obediently on a stool on the back verandah, while Piccolo puzzled over different solutions to the problem. The red frizzy stuff was water repellent, detergent repulsive, and as stiff as table legs. To separate the major strands he cleverly devised a web of ropes and weights until eventually Annabelle sat underneath a giant hairy starfish. Piccolo got to work combing and untangling with a gardening fork. He made a little progress, and found a spoon and a couple of his pencils, but after an hour Annabelle's head was sore and Piccolo's arms ached. He gave up.

'What if I sharpened the electric pruning shears, and just trimmed you a bit?' he suggested as he untied her.

In the end they decided to leave it to professionals, and made an appointment at L'Elegance Boutique in town.

'Oooh!' said Annabelle excitedly, 'it sounds so French and elegant! I used to be French, you know.'

'Of course you were,' said Piccolo reworking the timetable.

He made a little progress, and found a spoon.

There was time for a couple of painful performances of 'Waltzing Matilda' for earthly singing. By then, they both had just about had enough.

It was the end of the last day of the training programme. Tomorrow was the Inspection. Annabelle wilted onto the ottoman and Piccolo studied the lists. They contained mixed results. The 'Success/Failure' list had 'Yes/Maybe/Don't Know' columns.

Invisibility, for example, was in the Maybe column. Transformation was also a Maybe. After the beach ball incident she had managed to transform into a red-haired hamster type thing. At least it had legs. Piccolo had put a fairly firm tick under Yes for Mystification. A thorough job had been done on Kevin. Annabelle's general knowledge had improved slightly. She now believed that there had been human moon landings and, more strangely, that Australia has a queen. She could play 'Waltzing Matilda' on the harp, in both the heavenly and earthly versions.

These were things to be proud of, certainly. But there were too many Maybes, and there were still whole subjects under the Don't Know column. They had run out of time.

'Annabelle, shouldn't you do a bit more Angel Lore and Law before bed?'

Annabelle smiled wearily from the couch. 'Piccolo, you have been splendid and have done wonders, my love. You have transformed me from a dizzy ninny into a Princess of Guardian Angels,' she exaggerated. 'But truly we have done our best. We shall sleep on clouds tonight and have a peaceful and long breakfast tomorrow. Then there is the hairdresser at eleven. And what happens in the afternoon will happen.'

'The Inspection,' said Piccolo grimly.

'Snnnnoorrggfflllzzzz,' said Annabelle.

CHAPTER EIGHT
The Big Morning of the Big Day

Annabelle insisted they have their special breakfast in town. 'We'll sit in the sun and have a big, balanced breakfast at the Sunflower Café. We'll think about nothing and be refreshed.'

They caught the bus into Clearwater Bay, after chatting with the bus stop dog, and settled in at a table overlooking the water. Annabelle seemed calm and confident as she ordered her idea of a healthy balanced breakfast. She was the very picture of a normal great-aunt, with a bit of a hair problem. Piccolo tried to enjoy the sunshine on the little waves and his balanced meal, but he was nervous. Uninvited butterflies bounced around in his tummy. He played with his Banana Tempura—deep fried banana—chasing the pieces through cream. Annabelle chattered brightly until she noticed that Piccolo looked miserable and slightly green.

'Are you all right, precious. You don't look happy or well.'

'I'm OK. A bit nervous, I guess. Butterflies,' he said, smiling weakly.

'Oh, don't worry. Everything will be fine,' she said. But something began to nag at her unreliable memory.

'Hmmmm, "Happy and Well, Happy or Well" . . . that reminds me of something,' she muttered through a big mouthful of fried banana.

'That's it!' She swallowed. 'Guardee Happiness and Health. They test you on it. You are my Guardee. The Inspector will be checking to see if you are happy and healthy.' She looked at the greenish, miserable boy. 'You don't look too well, Piccolo, or very happy either.'

'I'll be all right. It's just all this cream mixed with nerves,' he said, playing with his bananas.

'Are you worried that I might fail after all our hard work and be sent away? Or are you worried that I might pass and stay to annoy you for ever?' Annabelle asked. Piccolo was confused by the question. He had been so caught up in his lists

and ticks and sharp HB pencils that he had forgotten why he was doing it.

'Um. Well yes, I mean no.'

'Look, Piccolo, don't worry either way. I will miss you terribly if I fail, but I'm a bouncy little person. I'll bounce back.' She demonstrated by hopping up and down in her seat. 'Oops, sorry, love.' The balanced breakfast was now mostly on the tablecloth and partly in his lap. They mopped up in silence.

Piccolo felt Annabelle deserved a better answer than 'Um yes no'.

'Of course, I want you to pass,' he said at last. 'I'll be happy and well by Inspection time.'

'Magnifique!' burst Annabelle. He still looked green and unconvincing to Annabelle, but she carried on her breakfast chatter as if she was as carefree as could be.

Annabelle's visit to the hairdressing salon was one of the happiest times in her life, and she said so loudly and often to the staff and other customers.

'It's my first time, you know, dear.'

The hairdresser found this easy to believe as she struggled with the tangled mass. Piccolo flipped through the piles of magazines then walked up and down the shopping mall. He wondered if he really did want Annabelle to stay in his fine old home for ever, or until his parents returned, or for another week. Was he feeling ill because she might pass or because she might fail? Today's Inspection felt as much like his own as Annabelle's. Piccolo had a serious fear of failing tests. He had never failed one in his life, and yet he often dreamt that he was at school, in his pyjamas, and failing.

Every half hour or so he looked in on his angel. The first hairdresser had collapsed in a heap, exhausted by the task and Annabelle's babbling stream of conversation. Her replacement was using an industrial strength carpet softener, and making progress.

Piccolo returned to his anxious wandering. The appointment had already gone an hour over time. He had not made a timetable for the day, but he had hoped to be at home by now. Some last minute revision and general tidying up would have been good, before 2.35 p.m. sharp— Inspection time. Looking vacantly in the window of Clapham's Stamps and Coins, he heard cheering from L'Elegance Boutique. He trotted back to find that Annabelle's hairdo was done. She walked out of the Boutique to rounds of applause, aglow with happiness and carrying a small bag of found objects. Piccolo was quite impressed. They had managed to tame the black-berry patch, and weld it into a big red beehive shape. It pulsed with energy, and might explode if provoked, but it was a more slightly normal looking great-aunt that skipped towards him.

'We don't need to go home just yet, do we? I'd like to try out my new hair for a while.'

Annabelle's hairdo was done.

Piccolo reluctantly agreed that an hour could be spared. He had just about given up on any final preparations.

The new hair worked well and did not explode. The strangers that Annabelle stopped agreed that it was a very fine 'do'. The local Sitting Member, a kind of politician, was wandering about the shopping mall. There was an election coming up.

What a nice happy man! thought Annabelle. He grinned continuously and gripped people by their hands. A film crew followed him closely. Annabelle caught up with him and gripped his hand, shaking it enthusiastically. It became a grinning competition, all taped for local television. Piccolo watched from behind a post.

'Could I live without her?' he wondered again.

Annabelle was now pointing and tilting her hair at the camera.

'Life would be peaceful, and predictable . . .

and maybe just a bit boring and lonely,' he had to admit.

The Sitting Member finally detached himself and scuttled away, wringing his stinging hand. Twenty-five minutes of their extra hour had passed. Annabelle was still having a lovely time and did not want to go home just yet.

'I feel wonderful! Chock full of confidence. How are you feeling now, dear?'

'Better, I think.'

'Excellent! Let's quickly buy something for the house! Liven it up a bit, for the Inspector.' They were walking past a shop calling itself 'Cactus Are Us—For All Your Spiky Needs' at the time.

'How about a nice tropical cactus?' suggested Annabelle and in she went.

'It should be "Cacti Are Us",' corrected Piccolo as he followed her inside, 'or "Cactus Is Us".' He liked words to be used properly.

CHAPTER NINE
Something Wicked That Way Went

'Do you see anything tropical, Piccolo? I'm not sure I like all these spiky ones. Excuse me, young missy. Do you have any without prickles?'

Piccolo inspected an interesting flowering Mexican cactus and wondered if he could enjoy collecting cacti. The shopkeeper was explaining the basic principles of the species to Annabelle.

'No, madam, there are no jungle cacti. They are a dry climate succul—'

There was an enormous crash through the front window of the shop and an entire van stopped halfway inside. Piccolo thought it was a bad parking accident until two men leapt out. They were wearing rubber masks and brandishing bats.

'Everyone on the floor! Don't move and you won't get biffed!' yelled the one with a cricket bat.

'You! Fat dame, with the hair. DOWN! NOW!' shouted the hockey stick man at Annabelle. She was so surprised that she could not move.

'Fat dame? Is he calling me a "fat dame", Piccolo?' Piccolo had to drag her onto the floor next to him. The thieves began loading pots into the van.

'Fancy ones. Just the fancy ones!' cried the cricket bat robber to the other.

They ran back and forth to the van with the rare prickly plunder.

'Ow, owey, ouch! These hurt! Why couldn't we do an orchid shop instead?' complained hockey stick robber.

'Get some help then! You! Kid with the fat dame! Give us a hand!' The cricket bat robber dragged Piccolo up by his tie. 'Put those in the truck! Move.'

Piccolo moved. There was no arguing to be done. Annabelle popped up after him.

'Do not call me fat and leave Piccolo alone!' she shouted. For her troubles she received a hockey stick in the hairdo. It exploded on impact, unravelling spectacularly and collected several spiky plants as Annabelle fell to the floor. Piccolo was busily and carefully ferrying cacti to the back of the van.

'My poor hair!' she wailed. 'Picking on Piccolo . . . these horrible dolts haven't met an angry invisible angel yet, have they,' Annabelle muttered angrily. She began straining and straining. Anger focused her attention. She was already transparent all over and a whole leg was missing by the time she heard sirens in the distance.

'Cops!' yelled the cricket bat robber. 'Go, go, go!'

The van doors were slammed shut. It rapidly reversed out of the smashed window.

'Wait! I haven't finished with you yet!' Annabelle yelled as she scrambled up, one-legged and shaking a transparent fist after the van.

'Look what they've done to my hair, Piccolo!' she wailed. 'Piccolo! Has anyone seen my boy?'

The staff and customers lay on the floor, too astonished by Annabelle's jellyfish appearance and missing leg to get up.

'He was still in the van, I think, when they shut the doors,' somebody said.

Annabelle ran out onto the footpath. She caught a glimpse of Piccolo through the back window as the van sped away. Releasing her transparent wings she flapped furiously after it. All thoughts of Angel Laws, of 'angelic secrecy and caution', and the Inspection were forgotten. Piccolo had been kidnapped!

*   *   *

Piccolo was highly uncomfortable bumping about in the back of the van. Things were worse at corners as rare and spiky cacti were hurled about. He looked out of the van window hoping to see the Clearwater Police close behind. Instead he saw a bobbing pink blur, coming closer and closer.

'Annabelle!' Piccolo shouted. This was definitely the most pleased he had ever been to see her. Excellent velocity, thought Piccolo the trainer, and good elevation. Oops! Annabelle had bounced off a building, but managed to correct her flight and stay on course. Good recovery.

When she clipped the town hall clock tower, Piccolo noticed that the time was eight minutes past two. 'I guess this means the Inspection is cancelled—after all that work.'

Annabelle was slowly catching up. Piccolo

Excellent velocity, thought Piccolo the trainer.

waved frantically as she drew level with the back of the van. He could see she was nearly bursting with her efforts. There was a bang as she landed on the roof. A transparent hand poked in through a hatch. He caught hold of it. 'I'll pull you out!' cried Annabelle. Piccolo was just beginning to wonder if this was a good plan when the van braked and swerved, narrowly avoiding a startled seagull. Their grip was broken. Annabelle flipped over onto the windscreen, grabbing a windscreen wiper.

'What in blue blazes is that?' yelled the driver.

'Get it off! Get it *off*! Turn on the wipers!'

Annabelle tightened her grip as she was sprayed and flung to and fro. Through the pink blur the driver failed to notice a red traffic light. There was a squealing and a crunching thud. The thieves sat stunned but undamaged. The wipers had slowed down, flipping a semi-conscious, semi-transparent Annabelle gently to and fro. The getaway vehicle had collided with another van, shaped like a giant cockroach. 'Purvis Pest Exterminators—Zap 'em Dead!' it read on the side. Annabelle was only centimetres away from the cockroach driver. She peered at him, dazed and rocking. The driver was a stern little man. He looked familiar. She was gazing into the eyes of her Inspector.

The Inspector, disguised as a pest exterminator, leapt out of his van. He heaved Annabelle from the windscreen wiper and bustled her vigorously into his van.

'Stay here!' he barked, rapidly putting on a backpack, hose, and mask. 'And stay out of sight! You're transparent, for Heaven's sake!'

He jogged the few metres to the robbers' van, sprayed them forcefully, then turned his attention to a crowd of onlookers.

Piccolo had tumbled gently out of the van in a porridge of broken pots, dirt, and squashed cacti. Folk had already moved him onto the footpath and had begun pulling out the biggest spines. He was trying to see what had become of Annabelle. Through the forest of legs he thought he saw her peering out of a brown van. A short stout man in a uniform and mask was running about spraying people with a hose.

'Sorry, folks!' he called. 'These are infectious cacti here. Bear with me while I disinfect . . .'

He didn't need to go on with his story. People all around were looking befuddled, slumping to the ground and nodding off. Piccolo suddenly realized that he was in the middle of a large-scale Mystification. He made himself look groggy, which was difficult, being full of prickles, and dropped painfully to the footpath. The man from the van quickly scanned his victims to make sure he hadn't missed any. An extra squirt was given to one or two of the tougher onlookers. Black boots crunched up close to Piccolo and paused. Piccolo felt that he was being checked especially carefully. Sirens were approaching.

The man ran back to the cockroach van, unstrapped his gear and drove smartly away.

'Annabelle, Annabelle,' sighed the Inspector, addressing his passenger and shaking his head. 'I am lost for words.'

'Is Piccolo all right?' she croaked pathetically.

'He will be fine.'

'Will you let me see him again before you send me away,' Annabelle pleaded tearfully.

'It is now 2.15 p.m.,' said the Inspector in a stern official tone. 'At 2.35, sharp, your Inspection will begin. But we have a lot to do before then.'

'You'll still Inspect me? Oh, thank you. Thank you so much, Inspector.'

'Save your thanks until you've passed, which would be a miracle of the large old-fashioned kind, looking at you now.' He looked at her with serious disapproval.

Annabelle twisted her ragged red hair and bounced about on exterminating gear. There's still hope! she thought. Not a lot, next to nought, probably hardly any, but some.

CHAPTER TEN
The Inspection

Piccolo waved to the ambulance as it drove away down the long gravel driveway. The nurses at the hospital had been very kind. They had pulled out his cactus spines, taped up all his scratches, checked him for leaks, and given him ice cream. A familiar cockroach-shaped van was parked by the front steps. Inside the house he could hear murmurings through the ballroom door. He knocked and went in. There was a stout man standing by the ottoman in the corner.

'Piccolo! Oh, you poor dear! Look at all those

plasters! Are you all right?' Annabelle cried as she rushed over and crushed him in a great hug. Letting him go at last, she rolled her eyes towards the man and mouthed 'Inspector'.

'I'm fine, Great-Auntie. Quite Happy and Healthy,' he said, a bit too loudly.

Annabelle introduced the Inspector as Mr Purvis. Mr Purvis carefully shook the boy's de-prickled hand. He was about Annabelle's height, but square rather than round, with a pencil-line moustache and plastered-down hair under his

cap. He wore a brown uniform and a serious frown behind heavy-rimmed glasses. There was a badge on his hat in the shape of an upside-down cockroach.

'Mr Purvis and I were just talking about those blessed white ants.' Annabelle turned to the Inspector and asked anxiously, 'Couldn't we do this some other time, Mr Purvis? This poor boy . . .'

'We-e-ell, Miss Grande . . .' Mr Purvis began slowly, pretending to read an appointment book. 'I have a very busy schedule . . . No, I'm afraid it's now or never, really . . .' He stared at her from under his heavy rims. Piccolo insisted again that he was feeling very happy and well, and that the termites needed finding—the sooner the better.

'I'll just lie down for a bit. It's been a very exciting day. My great-aunt rescued me from kidnapping robbers, you know.' He smiled encouragingly at his nervous angel, and left the room, closing the door behind him. Immediately he glued his wounded ear to the door. He could only hear mumblings and occasionally a clear word when the Inspector raised his voice. He tried to guess where they were up to. There was a clumsy plunk of harp strings and Annabelle's high, cracked voice.

'That's Singing. Flying should be next,' Piccolo reckoned.

After ten minutes of muffled song he heard a heavy thud followed by the tinkling of broken glass. 'Yes. That's Flying.'

As he strained listening at the door he noticed that his plasters were peeling off. He was sweating with anxiety. This is nerve-racking, he thought. I have to see what's going on. He crept outside and into a gardenia bush by one of the ballroom windows.

'I know you have been out of circulation for a long time, Annabelle . . .' said the Inspector. Piccolo could hear quite well now, but rustled further into his fragrant bush to get a better view.

'... but even you, *especially* you, should remember that it is illegal to impersonate an Inspector.'

Piccolo was confused for a moment. The Inspector was talking to another pest exterminator much like himself.

'Ah! Transformation,' Piccolo realized. 'Well done, Annabelle! That's your best ever. Pity it's illegal.'

Annabelle apologized profusely while straining to return to her own body.

'Moving on, we still have Angel Lore and Law, general knowledge, cooking ... you have prepared a dish, have you not?' She nodded blankly.

'And lastly, Guardee Health and Happiness.'

Annabelle's shoulders, already drooping, slumped further.

'"A dish"? She hasn't made a dish!' exclaimed Piccolo. 'I'll have to make something and quickly.' He backed out of the gardenias and trotted back inside to the kitchen. He looked about frantically.

'Lots of bananas, of course—banana cake? No time! Smoothie? That's not a "dish"! Um, um, think! Biscuits? That's sort of a "dish". Quicker in the microwave.'

Fifteen minutes later there was a mess in the kitchen that Annabelle would have been proud to call her own. Flour and skins and sugar and spices were strewn about. Tea was brewing. Piccolo rapidly assembled a tray.

'They must be halfway through general knowledge by now,' Piccolo estimated. 'Hurry up, microwave.'

Ding, it went. The biscuits smelt good but they looked limp.

'They need browning. Griller? Too slow! Blowtorch!'

Four more hurried minutes passed, involving a trip to his father's workshop, before the tray was assembled: tea in a sparkling pot, milk and sugar, a vase of gardenias, and nicely blowtorch-brown banana biscuits.

He stood with his tray and his ear against the ballroom door for a moment.

'. . . mumble mumble mumble cooking,' said the Inspector.

Now or never, thought Piccolo as he struggled with the tray and door knob.

'Excuse me!' Piccolo burst into the room, tray clattering, smiling brightly. 'I've just warmed up your biscuits, Great-Auntie. Mr Purvis, would you like to try some? Did you find the termites? How do you have your tea?' Annabelle grinned at her boy with gratitude, and admiration. What a clever tale teller he had suddenly become!

Afternoon tea was tense. The anxious angel ate an impolite number of biscuits. Piccolo chatted away, trying desperately to appear both happy and well. He described the wonderful trip to the zoo, how Great-Auntie had loved the lizards especially, and did Mr Purvis like lizards?

Were lizards ever pests? He hoped not because they were both very fond of them, and so on.

Annabelle was very quiet, apart from biscuit chewing and nervous tea slurping. She kept looking from the Inspector to Piccolo and back again. The talkative boy dropped a plate on purpose, to stop himself rabbiting on.

If this is the last part of the Inspection: Guardee Health and Happiness, thought Piccolo, then he must be wondering about my mental health. I sound like a complete idiot . . . Another plaster peeled off his face and fell to the floor. 'And I don't look healthy at all.'

After another endless silence, the Inspector 'ahemmed'.

'Well, thank you for the afternoon tea—and the conversation,' he said, smiling thinly. Slowly and deliberately he stood and opened his notebook.

'You have a serious pest problem here, I'm afraid, Miss Grande, Master Piccolo.'

Annabelle looked hard at a spot on the floor.

Piccolo tried to swallow the biscuit stuck in his throat.

'My first thought was that a Major Pest Problem needed to be eliminated immediately.' He glanced severely at Annabelle.

'However,' he paused, 'considering this, that, and the other, and after a careful look around,' another pause, 'I think your home will be safe for another three months. I am now making a note to return at that time.' He smiled humourlessly and snapped his notebook shut.

'Good day, Miss Grande, Master Piccolo.'

Piccolo and Annabelle scarcely breathed as they saw the Inspector to the door. He stopped by his cockroach van and called to Annabelle.

'May I have just one more word, Miss Grande—about the bill.'

Annabelle glanced at Piccolo, gripped by a sudden panic that the Inspector had changed his mind. She bustled down the steps and across the driveway. The Inspector turned with her and walked away crunching on the gravel. Piccolo strained, but could hear nothing.

'There was something strange about that robbery, Annabelle, and those thieves. I can't put my finger on it. I will do some investigating.'

The Inspector lowered his grim glasses and furrowed brow and looked into Annabelle's eyes. 'Meanwhile, until the next Inspection, you *must* take better care of Piccolo.'

'Yes, yes, of course. I won't let him out of my sight.'

He held her gaze a moment longer, and said 'Good.' He turned to his cockroach. 'Oh, and I had better give you a bill.'

Annabelle returned to Piccolo on the steps. Suddenly she felt extremely weary, and sat down with a flomph next to him. They watched the ugly brown van drive away.

'What was all that about?' asked Piccolo.

'Oh, just the bill. It's a complicated bill,' she

'What was that all about?' asked Piccolo.

said airily. She did not want to concern her worrying boy with the Inspector's suspicions.

'That Inspection was the worst time I've had in my extremely long life, almost,' she sighed heavily.

'But you did it, didn't you? You passed?' thinking that the bill conversation had gone on too long, and Annabelle might have failed after all.

'Yes! I did, didn't I? Thanks to you, I'm sure.' She looked at him and smiled gently. 'Are you completely sure you can stand me for another three months, at least?'

'Will you try to be as normal as possible, and not sing in public, and be polite to people in uniform?'

'Yes, yes, and I'll try.'

'Then I am happy to have you here. Anyway, somebody has to look after you.'

Annabelle's dam burst. There was a flood of hot pink tears. And then, of course, there was the pink smothering, only wetter this time, and shorter, as Piccolo squeaked and Annabelle remembered he was full of holes.

CHAPTER ELEVEN
A Beginning Again

The next morning they had their breakfast on the front verandah. It was a celebration breakfast on the plates for special occasions. These plates reminded Piccolo of happy birthdays past with his dear missing parents. But this morning he was too content to be sad. He sat by his great-aunt in the dappled sunshine. The scent of gardenias drifted sweetly. They ate their fresh fruit salad, toast with mango jam, and leftover biscuits and talked about their big day yesterday.

'What happened after you left the crash?' asked Piccolo.

'Let's see. I was in a bit of a state. Yes, we drove back along the route the robbers took. We must have stopped a dozen times. The Inspector Mystified a hundred people who might have seen me, even the police. They were at the cactus shop. "Oi!" said my big Sergeant Jim. "What in blue blazes are you up to, sir?" Squirt, squirt, and down he went too. I think he got everybody.'

'And after all that he still Inspected you. That wasn't fair. He should have postponed.'

'But he could have stripped me of my wings right then and there, Piccolo. It was good of him to Inspect me at all. I must have passed by the skin of my teeth, and you got me through, my brilliant boy. It was the biscuits that did it. How did you get them so toffee-like on top? Hmmm, yum.'

'My secret,' said Piccolo, choosing another one. 'Your transformation was pretty funny. I was peeking through the window.' Piccolo smiled.

'I saw you. You were lucky he didn't see you too. He has the eyes of an eagle and the ears of an elephant, only smaller,' Annabelle warned.

'He doesn't look much like an angel. He's too stiff,' said Piccolo.

'Oh yes, he's stiff all right. But what do you suppose angels look like? Do I look like an angel to you?'

Piccolo watched her poke another big biscuit into her pudding face. He looked at her tatty shawl and blazing, tangled hair.

'You're not quite what I imagined,' he agreed.

'Well, we come in all shapes, sizes, and colours . . . Oh! A visitor.'

They listened to the approaching crunch of gravel on the driveway.

'It's Henry, delivering the paper,' observed Piccolo. The small boy arrived, puffing, on his bike.

'You have a long driveway, Piccolo,' he pointed out, as he did every paper day.

'Yes I do, Henry,' agreed Piccolo, as *he* did every paper day.

Henry handed Piccolo his copy of the *Clearwater Klaxon*.

'Henry, this is my Great-Aunt Annabelle,' Piccolo said formally. Henry did not seem to recognize her, but he shook her hand warily.

'Will you have a cup of tea, dear, or a fruit

smoothie?' asked Annabelle. Henry looked at her carefully. He had an idea that there was something dangerous about Piccolo's great-aunt Annabelle.

'No thank you. I must deliver these before Sunday,' and off he crunched.

Piccolo found the front page, read a moment and burst out laughing. Annabelle smiled. He did not laugh very often and it warmed her heart to see him happy. He read out the headline.

'"Major Cactus Robbery Foiled! Young Kidnap Victim Found Prickled But Well." That's me!' He smiled and went on.

'"Bizarre Novelty B-B-Balloo . . ."' He had to stop due to an attack of merriment.

Annabelle took the paper from him.

'What's so funny? ". . . Prickled But Well . . . Bizarre Novelty Balloon and Roach Spray Win the Day! Witnesses report seeing a bizarre helium novelty balloon which seemed to be following the getaway van. Drinkers at the Bay

Hotel described it as a pink, winged baby elephant . . ." This is not funny. Not at all.'

Piccolo was laughing silently now, clutching his stomach, with tears streaming.

'Who wrote this rubbish? "By Erica Stringer". Typical,' Annabelle humphed.

Piccolo struggled back into his chair. He felt lighter and happier than he could remember, despite the stomach cramps.

'I'm sorry, Annabelle. Keep reading,' he wheezed.

'It goes on about the crash . . . dum de dum . . . yes, "Police are anxious to interview the driver of a cockroach-styled van who may be able to assist them with their enquiries." The Inspector must have missed some witnesses. He will have to get rid of that ugly van and change his disguise.'

In the morning sunshine, full of special breakfast and still glowing from laughter, Piccolo realized that he had not been so happy since his dear parents were lost. His life without them had been orderly and calm, but lonely and colourless too. There had been no dramas or embarrassments, and no danger or lying, but there hadn't been any laughter either. He looked over at his roly-poly angel with her flaming red hair and made a decision.

'Let's go for a walk, Annabelle,' he suggested. He led her into the back garden, past the orange orchard to the grove of lillypilly trees.

'Where are you taking me? I've eaten too much,' she grumbled.

'It's just in here,' said Piccolo as they ducked their heads and stepped into his special place.

'Oh, Piccolo! What a lovely spot!'

Piccolo sat down at the edge of the pond and put his feet in. 'Come and meet Mum and Dad.'

Annabelle joined Piccolo and put her feet in too. The two perch swam to the strange chubby feet and gave them a good exploratory nibbling. 'How delightful!' she giggled.

'Mum, Dad, meet Annabelle. The pretty one on the left is Mum,' he explained.

Mum and Dad perch were wide-eyed with delight to be meeting Piccolo's new friend.

'I come here when I need to talk to someone. No one's ever been here except my real mum and dad, and me.'

'Thank you, Piccolo. You're a darling to bring me and I'm honoured.'

They enjoyed the fishy foot chewing for a while in silence.

Piccolo pulled out a little notebook and pen from his shirt pocket. With his capable, serious face on, he said, 'Well, we'd better start on the training schedule for the next Inspection, which is only two months, three weeks, six days, and twenty-one hours away. Let's say we have the rest of today off, then get started in the morning . . . What's the matter?' Annabelle was staring at him, horrified.

'No! Not so soon, surely. We've got *three* months!'

The perch watched the struggle above them.

'No. Two months, three weeks . . .'

The weary angel groaned.

'We'll start with Identifying Termites,' continued bossy Piccolo, 'then Novelty Balloon Animals, How to Buy a Cactus,' he listed, with a straight face, 'then Cake Burning . . .'

'Oh! You! You junior demon!' cried Annabelle, grinning with relief. 'You're pulling my leg!'

Piccolo was chuckling hard, very amused by his own drollery. Annabelle clutched her boy, not for a tearful smothering this time, but for a serious tickling.

The perch watched the struggle above them, leaping in and out of the water, their eyes wide with glee.

THE
END

The mysterious visitor and her long-armed driver

COMING SOON . . .

PICCOLO AND ANNABELLE
VOLUME TWO

A DISASTROUS PARTY

Great-Aunt Annabelle has passed her very messy inspection and can stay on as Piccolo's Guardian Angel—for now. But with a new-found passion for winning competitions, will Annabelle be too busy to notice if Piccolo is in danger?

When Annabelle wins a party, who is the beautiful but mysterious visitor who arrives unannounced in a sleek silver limousine—is she friend or foe, angel or otherwise? Only A Disastrous Party *will reveal her secrets and Annabelle's curious past.*

What follows is a tantalizing taste of Volume Two . . .

Great-Aunt Annabelle's new hobby was winning things. She had incredible luck with every kind of raffle, lottery, and guessing competition. She bustled about the big kitchen table delving into great messy piles of magazines, letters, cut-out entry forms, scribblings, and label collections. In the last week alone she had won a year's supply of dog food, a trampoline, and a tip-truck load of money. The trampoline would be useful, thought Piccolo, for her flying lessons, if she ever went back into training. The money was safe in the cellar vault. This might be useful one day. They did not need the dog food. His only pets were Mum and Dad, his two special perch.

Piccolo sighed. He carefully gathered his beloved but boring stamps and put them away in a cupboard.

'I'll see you soon, don't worry,' he reassured them as he closed the door, then wondered if he would. He went downstairs to the ball-room to bounce away his boredom on the prize trampoline. As he bounced and flipped, he wondered again if Annabelle had some angelic way of cheating. She seemed to be supernaturally lucky.

Surely not, he thought, somersaulting cleverly. There would be rules about angels cheating. Angels have such a lot of strict rules.

His doubts and suspicions were cut short by an 'AAAAAGH!' from the kitchen. The scream made him miss a flip and he landed badly on the edge of the trampoline. Annabelle burst into the ballroom. Piccolo was doubled up, breathing heavily.

'I've won! I've won,' she bellowed joyously.

'You always win,' said Piccolo between his knees.

'Yes, but this time it was *skill*, not dumb luck! Are you all right, dear?'

'I'll be fine,' he wheezed. 'What did you win?'

'Remember my Party People jingle?'

If you're ninety-eight and shaky,
or if you're just sixteen and flaky,

'I've won, I've won,' she bellowed joyously.

be you glum or hale and hearty,
it's always time to throw a party!

We've won a party, Piccolo!'

Piccolo tried to smile, but he was not happy. A party person he was not. Annabelle most definitely was. She skipped about with excitement.

'We can have it anywhere, any time! They provide food and tents and costumes and rides— even stamps and envelopes for invitations! We'll invite everyone! Here! We'll have it here, yes?'

'Or how about the dark side of the moon?' said Piccolo, but his Guardian Angel was not listening, and missed his gloomy suggestion.

'We'll celebrate us, you and me, living happy as geese in a tree!' she trilled, and chatted on rapidly about the great joys to come, for one and all, and others as well.

Oh, dear. We're having a party, thought Piccolo miserably. So very, very many things could go wrong.

ABOUT STEPHEN AXELSEN

Born in Sydney a long time ago, Stephen has illustrated hundreds of children's stories and cartoon strips since 1974 and this is his third book as author and illustrator.

Stephen lives by the beach, watching the tides, near Byron Bay with his wife, Jennifer, and two big children, Lauren and Harlee. They share their house with a dog named Oscar, a cat called Willow, and their budgie, Trippy. When not illustrating or writing, Stephen might be found gardening, walking Oscar, or reading until he falls asleep. He also hunts cane toads on summer nights, but not for pleasure!

Acknowledgements

I would like to thank Ali Lavau for telling me to have a go, Rosalind Price for telling me to keep going, Eva Mills for saying 'Let's go!', my dad for saying 'So all this came out of your head, did it?' and Heather Curdie for the nurturing.